The Secret of Hanging Rock

The Secret of Hanging Rock

Joan Lindsay's final chapter
with an introduction by John Taylor
and a commentary by Yvonne Rousseau

ANGUS
& ROBERTSON
PUBLISHERS

ANGUS & ROBERTSON PUBLISHERS

Unit 4, Eden Park, 31 Waterloo Road,
North Ryde, NSW, Australia 2113, and
16 Golden Square, London W1R 4BN,
United Kingdom

First published in Australia
by Angus & Robertson Publishers in 1987
First published in the United Kingdom
by Angus & Robertson UK in 1987
Reprinted 1987

National Library of Australia
Cataloguing-in-publication data.

Lindsay, Joan, 1896-1984.
    The secret of Hanging Rock.

    ISBN 0 207 15550 X.

    I. Rousseau, Yvonne. II. Lindsay, Joan, 1896-1984.
    Picnic at Hanging Rock. III. Title. IV. Title:
    Picnic at Hanging Rock.

A823'.3

Typeset in 14/16 Bem Expanded by Midland Typesetters
Printed in Australia

Contents

Introduction

Joan Lindsay's *Picnic at Hanging Rock* has been read by several million people in English, French, Spanish and Italian, and the film version seen by tens of millions.

As a novel its appeal came chiefly from two things: the way it combined mysterious and sinister events with a picture of a period drawn with loving nostalgia, and the fact that the mystery was left unsolved.

The central story can be briefly summarised. A party of schoolgirls goes on a picnic on St Valentine's Day, 1900. Four of them leave the group to explore the Hanging Rock. One of the schoolmistresses also wanders off. When they do not return in time, a search is organised. The youngest girl emerges from the hillside in hysterics, but can recall almost nothing. Of the other three girls and the mistress there is no trace. A week later, one of the girls is found on the rock with a few cuts and bruises on her hands and face, but her bare feet unmarked and no memory of where she has been.

Such an unlikely plot could never work except in the hands of a writer of remarkable talent. It is perhaps because we are so convinced of the reality of the time, place and people that we can accept the mystery for what it is. Joan Lindsay wrote with a sharpness of observation, a shrewdness of insight and a humour which carry us to the puzzling conclusion. We do not feel cheated, because such a writer doesn't cheat.

There have been attempts to "explain" the unsolved mystery by suggesting that it was derived from, or inspired by, the Marabar Caves incident in E. M. Forster's *A Passage to India*, or an apparently bogus incident described in a book called *The Ghosts of Versailles*. There is no evidence that Joan Lindsay ever read either book. Her own account was that the story "just came to her" in stages as she lay awake at night, to be written at high speed the next day.

But what came to her did include the ending, and although we were not cheated, we were misled.

Joan Lindsay kept silent on the subject of the final chapter for the sake of her publishers and the film-makers. However, she expressed a clear wish that it should be published after her death. In the light of this, it seems absurd that many people have argued that it should not be published, as though they had a better knowledge than the author, or a right to overrule her.

However, many thousands of others have begged to know the secret, and they have it now with the author's consent.

When, to please her publisher, Joan Lindsay agreed to remove the final chapter, it was not the only change she made.

At the beginning of the novel there is a note by the author:

Whether *Picnic at Hanging Rock* is Fact or Fiction, my readers must decide for themselves. As the fateful picnic took place in the year nineteen hundred, and all the characters who appear in this book are long since dead, it hardly seems important.

But after writing it, she altered it to read "Fact or Fiction or both". The words were never included, but one can ponder them.

Many people have spent many hours

searching through old newspapers and records, hoping to find the "facts". Yvonne Rousseau, in her remarkable scholarly spoof *The Murders at Hanging Rock*, showed that an astonishing number of "solutions" could be made to seem plausible by combining fact with fiction. She put her finger on the fundamental fact that the supposed date of the picnic was not a Saturday, as the author said, but a Wednesday.

Picnic at Hanging Rock is remarkable for the fact that it is the only one of Joan Lindsay's works to contain any dates at all. One should not be surprised to find them ambiguous.

The Invisible
Foundation Stone

JOHN TAYLOR

Chapter Eighteen of *Picnic at Hanging Rock* has been the subject of a great deal of nonsense.

Joan Lindsay wrote it as part of her novel, intending it to be published. Whether it would have "spoiled" the story to include it is a question for each reader to decide. The publishers' readers thought it should be deleted. It was a purely literary decision, but historians might well decide that its indirect result was the creation of the Australian film industry as we know it — because it is highly unlikely that there would have been a rush to buy the film rights in 1972 if Chapter Eighteen had not been deleted.

As anyone can see, the chapter is quite unfilmable. Film can work only with what God gives it, and God did not give it the same elasticity He granted the novel — though people keep trying, as the cutting-room floor forever shows.

I understand that one of the greatest sequences ever filmed was Mrs Appleyard rushing up the Hanging Rock between a raging bushfire and an approaching thunderstorm, on her way to commit suicide.

But God had decreed that you can show just so many people climbing a given Rock in one picture, and the editor's decision was final. What we saw was a subtitle.

Joan gave me the manuscript of Chapter Eighteen in December 1972, to my considerable surprise.

As Promotions Manager for her publisher (Cheshire, Melbourne), I had the unwelcome task of dealing with the various people who were seeking to buy the film rights. It was not part of my job, and I knew little about it. Eventually, I observed that Pat Lovell and Peter Weir were the best contenders, and I took them to meet Lady Lindsay at her house, Mulberry Hill.

As usual with Joan, she made up her mind instantly that they were the right people, and we might as well have left after five minutes. However, we spent a pleasant afternoon chatting and looking at her pictures and being charmed by her—an effect she produced without the slightest effort or artifice.

Being a professional publishing person, I naturally hadn't actually read the book.

People in publishing rarely have time to read anything—a fact that accounts for much of the tension which arises between them and authors. Publishers refer to books as "titles" and collectively as "lists". Lists of titles are what publishing is about. Actual pages of print are too time-consuming.

I was therefore puzzled by some of the conversation, which was about some kind of unsolved mystery. I nodded wisely, and told myself I had better get hold of a copy and read it over the weekend, which I did.

The next time I saw Joan, I mentioned that I had noticed a few things that didn't add up, and had drawn some conclusions. "Ah," she said. "You're one of very few people who've noticed that." I felt pleased that I had joined a small club.

A few months later Joan took me aside after lunch at her club with some of her friends. She produced the wad of manuscript and said, "I'm giving this to you because you're the only one who ever worked out the secret."

"But Lady —— just told me at lunch that *she* knew the secret," I protested.

"Oh, she didn't work it out," said Joan. "She just nagged and nagged and I had to tell her." Well, they were old friends.

What had I worked out? Nothing much more than that some words in Chapter Three didn't seem to fit—that the references to "drifts of rosy smoke" and "the beating of far-off drums" seemed to anticipate later events and that the author appeared to be playing tricks with time.

As is now clear, some sections of Chapter Eighteen were transferred (not very expertly) to Chapter Three.

The manuscript used by the editor and typesetter has not survived, so one cannot examine the method by which this was done. With hindsight, it looks like a scissors-and-paste job rather than a rewriting of the chapter.

(Between reading the book and discussing my observations with the author, I tried to find the manuscript. I was told that it was in the warehouse—but when I called for it, I was told it had gone to the pulpers along with the various unsaleable books which from time to time went to the cardboard manufacturers. In those days publishers were under the impression that they owned the manuscripts from which they published. The Moorhouse judgment changed that idea — too late in this case.)

So far as I know, Joan's method was to write in longhand, then type a draft, and perhaps a second draft. I don't know of any surviving longhand drafts — she and Sir Daryl used to have bonfires of unwanted papers and drawings, and no doubt the handwritten version perished in this way. Chapter Eighteen is from a typed draft, and presumably was never revised. The manuscript from which the book was published might have been a further revision — though how much of it was revised one doesn't know.

That she made carbon copies of the first typed draft is evident from the fact that a copy of Chapter Eighteen turned up among her papers, which were inherited with the contents of Mulberry Hill by the National Trust.

In *The Murders at Hanging Rock* (1980), Yvonne Rousseau, working from the published version as we know it, profited greatly from various anomalies others had overlooked.

I have never met Ms Rousseau, and I am not sure that I want to—she makes Sherlock Holmes look like an amateur, and such people can be unnerving. Like Sherlock Holmes, she had to work backwards (which is the way Conan Doyle constructed the stories—first the solution, then the mystery).

With no solution to start from, she worked backwards from what the text appeared to be saying, which is often not what the author intended. It is unfortunate that Ms Rousseau was deprived of the pleasure I had in being the first to spot the bits of Chapter Three which don't quite fit. To my lasting regret, I revealed the place where clues lie to a Melbourne journalist in 1975—and the world has never heard the end of his "solution".

Still, I yield all honour to Ms Rousseau—if she makes Holmes look amateurish, she makes me look feeble-minded. I advise anyone who hasn't done so to read *The Murders at Hanging Rock*. To produce five equally convincing and totally contradictory "solutions" to a mystery which was never meant to be a mystery (except in so far as Chapter Eighteen *is* mysterious) is an astonishing achievement.

Almost anyone living in Australia heard the stories circulated in the media in early February 1985 about the "revelation" that Chapter Eighteen existed.

Journalism is not an exact art, but there was something almost awe-inspiring about the way a few simple facts were transmogrified into a mass of confusion. I found myself being quoted saying things I would deny to the death, talking unscientific rubbish about "time zones" and agreeing with the views of people I knew to be entirely wrong.

The general impression that Chapter Eighteen either didn't exist, or was a forgery, or was public property which I had purloined for my own benefit will quite probably survive in the newspaper files long after these present words are forgotten.

Joan gave me the copyright, to be used at my discretion after her death (she was 84 at the time), as part of her general horrified reaction to the flood of demanding inquiries which came to her, especially after the film was made. Each time the phony "solution" was trumpeted in a newspaper, the flood would increase. Being by this time her literary agent, I had to deal with them—by merely saying that Lady Lindsay did not care to discuss the matter.

Although she knew perfectly well that the huge success of both book and film had a lot to do with the mystery of "what really happened", she had moments of wishing she had published the final chapter and saved herself the pestering.

She was equally irritated by demands to know whether the novel was based on "real" events. Any artist is insulted by the suggestion that art is merely a matter of recording reality, and knows that it is impossible to explain how imagination can transform not only events and people, but the artist as well, into quite different "realities".

But beyond that, reality had a way of behaving a little differently towards Joan. She could not wear a watch, because watches tended to stop — not only on her, but on people around her. She thought it absurd to wear a wedding ring — so a bird obligingly flew in the window and carried hers off to its nest in a tall pine (where it may be still).

I don't know whether she has recorded the anecdote elsewhere, but she once told me that in about 1929 her husband was driving her to Creswick to dine with his mother when Joan observed a strange sight: half a dozen nuns were running frantically across a field and climbing a fence. Her husband saw nothing. Puzzled, she asked her mother-in-law if there was a convent in the area. There had been, she was told, but it had burned down years earlier.

(Years later, in London, her cousin Martin Boyd was bemoaning the fact that he was contracted to write a novel but had no ideas — not even for a title: could she suggest one? "*Nuns in Jeopardy*," said Joan, and it was enough.)

With reality like that, and the pride of an artist who has produced a unique work, it is not surprising that she wished everybody would accept the work for what it was and not bother her.

But one day she handed me some more letters from people who had been researching fruitlessly through old newspapers, hoping to find the "real" events. I remarked that it was sad they wasted so much time. "Yes," said Joan—and then, absently, "but something did happen."

Whether the something happened in the newspapers, in some anecdote she had heard or in her imagination's interconnections with some other world or time, I had no idea—and I knew better than to ask.

Certainly she *wanted* Chapter Eighteen to appear. What artist wants to conceal an unflawed work? She came, I think, to feel that it would be better not *printed*. She was meticulous in respecting the interests of those who were exploiting her work, and understood that it might have worked against those interests. That is no longer the case.

Here, then, is the previously invisible foundation stone on whose absence the Australian film industry built itself.

The stone which the builders rejected
is become the corner of the temple.
(Psalm CXVIII)

And for what they have received, may St Valentine make the film producers and Commissions of Australia truly thankful.

THE CHARACTERS MENTIONED

Miranda
The most popular student at Appleyard College,
fair-haired and slender,
like a "Botticelli angel"

Irma Leopold
The wealthiest student at the College,
with "full red lips, naughty black eyes
and glossy black ringlets"

Marion Quade
The cleverest student at the College,
with "thin intelligent features"

Edith Horton
The College dunce, "plain as a frog",
"with the contours of an overstuffed bolster"

Miss Greta McCraw
The College mathematics teacher,
"a tall woman with dry ochre skin
and coarse greying hair"

Mrs Appleyard
The principal of Appleyard College,
"an immense purposeful figure . . .
like a galleon in full sail"

The Hon. Michael Fitzhubert
The English nephew
of Colonel and Mrs Fitzhubert of Lake View,
"a slender fair youth"

Chapter Eighteen

JOAN LINDSAY

It is happening now. As it has been happening ever since Edith Horton ran stumbling and screaming towards the plain. As it will go on happening until the end of time. The scene is never varied by so much as the falling of a leaf or the flight of a bird. To the four people on the Rock it is always acted out in the tepid twilight of a present without a past. Their joys and agonies are forever new.

Miranda is a little ahead of Irma and Marion as they push on through the dogwoods, her straight yellow hair swinging loose as cornsilk about her thrusting shoulders. Like a swimmer, cleaving wave after wave of dusty green. An eagle hovering in the zenith sees an unaccustomed stirring of lighter patches amongst the scrub below, and takes off for higher, purer airs. At last the bushes are thinning out before the face of a little cliff that holds the last light of the sun. So on a million summer evenings the pattern forms and re-forms upon the crags and pinnacles of the Hanging Rock.

The plateau on which they presently emerged from the scrub had much the same confor-

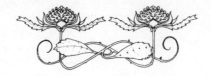

mation as the one lower down—boulders, loose stones, an occasional stunted tree. Clumps of rubbery ferns stirred faintly in the pale light. The plain below was infinitely vague and distant. Peering down between the ringing boulders, they could just make out tiny figures coming and going, through drifts of rosy smoke. A dark shape that might have been a vehicle beside the glint of water.

"Whatever can those people be doing down there, scuttling about like a lot of busy little ants?" Marion came and looked over Irma's shoulder. "A surprising number of human beings are without purpose." Irma giggled. "I dare say they think themselves quite important."

The ants and their fires were dismissed without further comment. Although Irma was aware, for a little while, of a rather curious sound coming up from the plain, like the beating of far-off drums.

Miranda had been the first to see the monolith—a single outcrop of stone something like a monstrous egg, rising smoothly out of the rocks ahead above a precipitous drop to the plain. Irma, a few feet

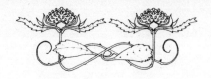

behind the other two, saw them suddenly halt, swaying a little, with heads bent and hands pressed to their breasts as if to steady themselves against a gale.

"What is it, Marion? Is anything the matter?"

Marion's eyes were fixed and brilliant, her nostrils dilated, and Irma thought vaguely how like a greyhound she was.

"Irma! Don't you feel it?"

"Feel what, Marion?" Not a twig was stirring on the little dried-up trees.

"The monolith. Pulling, like a tide. It's just about pulling me inside out, if you want to know." As Marion Quade seldom joked, Irma was afraid to smile. Especially as Miranda was calling back over her shoulder, "What side do you feel it strongest, Marion?"

"I can't make it out. We seem to be spiralling on the surface of a cone—all directions at once." Mathematics again! When Marion Quade was particularly silly it was usually something to do with sums. Irma said lightly, "Sounds to me more like a circus! Come on, girls—we don't want to stand staring at that great thing forever."

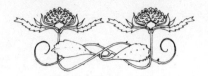

As soon as the monolith was passed and out of sight, all three were overcome by an overpowering drowsiness. Lying down in a row on the smooth floor of a little plateau, they fell into a sleep so deep that a lizard darted out from under a rock and lay without fear in the hollow of Marion's outflung arm, while several beetles in bronze armour made a leisurely tour of Miranda's yellow head.

Miranda awoke first, to a colourless twilight in which every detail was intensified, every object clearly defined and separate. A forsaken nest wedged in the fork of a long-dead tree, with every straw and feather intricately laced and woven; Marion's torn muslin skirts fluted like a shell; Irma's dark ringlets standing away from her face in exquisite wiry confusion, the eyelashes drawn in bold sweeps on the cheek-bones. Everything, if you could only see it clearly enough, like this, is beautiful and complete. Everything has its own perfection.

A little brown snake dragging its scaly body across the gravel made a sound like wind passing over the ground. The whole air was clamorous with microscopic life.

Irma and Marion were still asleep. Miranda could hear the separate beating of their two hearts, like two little drums, each at a different tempo. And in the undergrowth beyond the clearing a crackling and snapping of twigs where a living creature moved unseen towards them through the scrub. It drew nearer, the crunchings and cracklings split the silence as the bushes were pushed violently apart and a heavy object was propelled from the undergrowth almost on to Miranda's lap.

It was a woman with a gaunt, raddled face trimmed with bushy black eyebrows — a clown-like figure dressed in a torn calico camisole and long calico drawers frilled below the knees of two stick-like legs, feebly kicking out in black lace-up boots.

"Through!" gasped the wide-open mouth, and again, "Through!" The tousled head fell sideways, the hooded eyes closed. "Poor thing! She looks ill," Irma said. "Where does she come from?"

"Put your arm under her head," Miranda said, "while I unlace her stays."

Freed from the confining husks, with her head pillowed on a folded petticoat, the

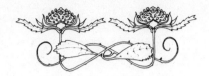

stranger's breath became regular, the strained expression left her face and presently she rolled over on the rock and slept.

"Why don't we all get out of these absurd garments?" Marion asked. "After all, we have plenty of ribs to keep us vertical."

No sooner were the four pairs of corsets discarded on the stones and a delightful coolness and freedom set in, than Marion's sense of order was affronted. "Everything in the universe has its appointed place, beginning with the plants. Yes, Irma, I meant it. You needn't giggle. Even our corsets on the Hanging Rock."

"Well, you won't find a wardrobe," Irma said, "however hard you look. Where can we put them?" Miranda suggested throwing them over the precipice. "Give them to me."

"Which way did they fall?" Marion wanted to know. "I was standing right beside you but I couldn't tell."

"You didn't see them fall because they *didn't* fall." The precise croaking voice came at them like a trumpet from the mouth of the clown-woman on the rock, now sitting

up and looking perfectly comfortable. "I think, girl, that if you turn your head to the right and look about level with your waist . . ." They all turned their heads to the right and there, sure enough, were the corsets, becalmed on the windless air like a fleet of little ships. Miranda had picked up a dead branch, long enough to reach them, and was lashing out at the stupid things seemingly glued to the background of grey air.

"Let me try!" Marion said. Whack! Whack! "They must be stuck fast in something I can't see."

"If you want my opinion," croaked the stranger, "they are stuck fast in *time*. You with the curls—what are you staring at?"

"I didn't mean to stare. Only when you said that about *time* I had such a funny feeling I had met you somewhere. A long time ago."

"Anything is possible, unless it is proved impossible. And sometimes even then." The scratchy voice had a convincing ring of authority. "And now, since we seem to be thrown together on a plane of common experience—I have no idea why—may I have your names? I have apparently left my own

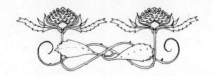

particular label somewhere over there." She waved towards the blank wall of scrub. "No matter. I perceive that I have discarded a good deal of clothing. However, here I am. The pressure on my physical body must have been very severe." She passed a hand over her eyes and Marion asked with a strange humility, "Do you suggest we should go on before the light fades?"

"For a person of your intelligence—I can see your brain quite distinctly—you are not very observant. Since there are no shadows here, the light too is unchanging."

Irma was looking worried. "I don't understand. Please, does that mean that if there are caves, they are filled with light or darkness? I am terrified of bats."

Miranda was radiant. "Irma, darling—don't you see? It means we arrive in the light!"

"Arrive? But Miranda . . . where are we going?"

"The girl Miranda is correct. I can see her heart, and it is full of understanding. Every living creature is due to arrive somewhere. If I know nothing else, at least I know that." She had risen to her feet, and

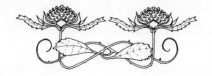

for a moment they thought she looked almost beautiful. "Actually, I think we *are* arriving. Now." A sudden giddiness set her whole being spinning like a top. It passed, and she saw the hole ahead.

It wasn't a hole in the rocks, nor a hole in the ground. It was a hole in space. About the size of a fully rounded summer moon, coming and going. She saw it as painters and sculptors saw a hole, as a thing in itself, giving shape and significance to other shapes. As a presence, not an absence—a concrete affirmation of truth. She felt that she could go on looking at it forever in wonder and delight, from above, from below, from the other side. It was as solid as the globe, as transparent as an air-bubble. An opening, easily passed through, and yet not concave at all.

She had passed a lifetime asking questions and now they were answered, simply by looking at the hole. It faded out, and at last she was at peace.

The little brown snake had appeared again and was lying beside a crack that ran off somewhere underneath the lower of two enormous boulders balancing one on top of

the other. When Miranda bent down and touched its exquisitely patterned scales it slithered away into a tangle of giant vines. Marion knelt down beside her and together they began tearing away the loose gravel and the tangled cables of the vine.

"It went down there. Look, Miranda—down that opening." A hole—perhaps the lip of a cave or tunnel, rimmed with bruised, heart-shaped leaves.

"You'll agree it's my privilege to enter first?"

"To enter?" they said, looking from the narrow lip of the cave to the wide, angular hips.

"Quite simple. You are thinking in terms of linear measurements, girl Marion. When I give you the signal—probably a tap on the rock—you may follow me, and the girl Miranda can follow you. Is that clearly understood?" The raddled face was radiant.

Before anyone could answer, the long-boned torso was flattening itself out on the ground beside the hole, deliberately forming itself to the needs of a creature created to creep and burrow under the earth. The thin arms, crossed behind the head with its bright staring

eyes, became the pincers of a giant crab that inhabits mud-caked billabongs. Slowly the body dragged itself inch by inch through the hole. First the head vanished; then the shoulder-blades humped together; the frilled pantaloons, the long black sticks of the legs welded together like a tail ending in two black boots.

"I can hardly wait for the signal," Marion said. When presently a few firm raps were heard from under the rock she went in quite easily, head first, smoothing down her chemise without a backward glance. "My turn next," Miranda said. Irma looked at Miranda kneeling beside the hole, her bare feet embedded in vine leaves — so calm, so beautiful, so unafraid. "Oh, Miranda, darling Miranda, don't go down there — I'm frightened. Let's go home!"

"Home? I don't understand, my little love. Why are you crying? Listen! Is that Marion tapping? I must go." Her eyes shone like stars. The tapping came again. Miranda pulled her long, lovely legs after her and was gone.

Irma sat down on a rock to wait. A

procession of tiny insects was winding through a wilderness of dry moss. Where had they come from? Where were they going? Where was anyone going? Why, oh why, had Miranda thrust her bright head into a dark hole in the ground? She looked up at the colourless grey sky, at the drab, rubbery ferns, and sobbed aloud.

How long had she been staring at the lip of the cave, staring and listening for Miranda to tap on the rock? Listening and staring, staring and listening. Two or three runnels of loose sand came pattering down the lower of the two great boulders on to the flat upturned leaves of the vine as it tilted slowly forward and sank with a sickening precision directly over the hole.

Irma had flung herself down on the rocks and was tearing and beating at the gritty face of the boulder with her bare hands. She had always been clever at embroidery. They were pretty little hands, soft and white.

END

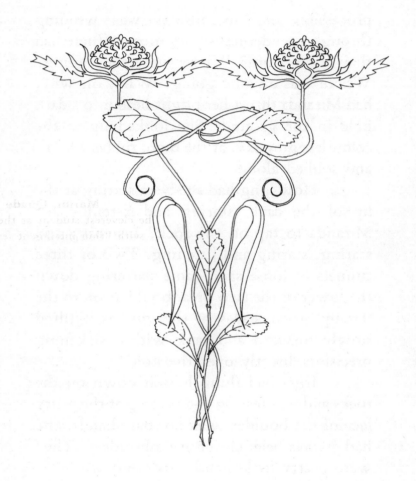

A Commentary on Chapter Eighteen

YVONNE ROUSSEAU

Joan Lindsay agreed with her editor that *Picnic at Hanging Rock* would be published without its original Chapter Eighteen. To make up for the loss of information, changes had to be made to the original Chapter Three, where the girls on the Rock went out of view. As an incidental result of these changes, another slope and a belt of dogwoods were added to the scene; thus making things difficult for visitors to Hanging Rock who wanted to map the path described in the book. A notebook and pencil belonging to Marion were also added, only to be thrown into some ferns near the monolith and never found again, even by the police bloodhound.

In both versions, Irma and Marion and Miranda are accompanied part way up the Rock by Edith Horton, a younger girl, who is known as the school dunce, and who thinks that the Rock is nasty. If we reconstruct the original Chapter Three on the assumption that as few changes as possible would have been made, then in both versions the girls decide to rest in the shade on an almost circular platform. In both versions their experience becomes strange at this point. The three older girls take off their shoes and stockings, and Irma dances barefoot on the stones. She is still barefooted when she is found on the Rock eight days later, but her feet are "perfectly clean" and "in no way scratched or bruised".[1] Thus, the Rock has become in some way insulated from these humans; its dust is not disturbed by their movement, its stones will not be overturned or bloodstained by anything they do. But only the living flesh seems to be set apart in this way; in both versions, the dead vegetable fibres of the girls' muslin and calico get torn by the dogwoods, although we may assume that their faces and hands, like their feet, are not scratched.

After the dancing, Miranda and Marion set off, barefooted, up the next little rise. Edith draws Irma's attention to their lunacy. Irma only laughs, slings her shoes and stockings about her waist, and sets off after them. In the original version, it will have been here that Edith makes her last attempt to recall them. She asks Miranda, "When are we going home?" But Miranda only looks at her strangely, as if not seeing her; then turns her back, and leads the other two on up the rise.

Edith sees them "sliding over the stones on their bare feet as if they were on a drawing-room carpet".[2] Half-petrified, she croaks Miranda's name several times as they move into some dogwoods and out of sight; until she sees "the last of a white sleeve parting the bushes ahead". An "awful silence" descends, and Edith begins to scream. She runs, still screaming, back down towards the plain; and the author assures us that her screams are heard only by a nearby wallaby.

In the published version, the little rise with the dogwoods becomes two rises and two sets of dogwoods. Between the appeal to Irma and the appeal to Miranda, some of the material from Chapter Eighteen has been inserted, and changed. This time Edith has continued trudging along behind the others. She is there when Irma looks down towards the plain and sees some "rosy smoke, or mist" and some people who seem so far away that they look like ants.[3] Edith falls asleep with the others too; but in the published version — the altered Chapter Three — their sleeping occurs on the plateau where the monolith is, instead of on the next plateau, near the

Balancing Boulders. When they wake, Edith makes her final appeal to Miranda, with the same results as in the original version. But the topography has become strangely confused — the three older girls are moving up a rise and into some bushes, but also "out of sight behind the monolith" at the same time.[4]

Chapter Eighteen belongs to the original version, where Edith ran away without climbing further than the platform where Irma danced. An eagle is hovering in the sky as the three other girls approach the monolith — just as an eagle will hover above, forty days later, when Mrs Appleyard (the College principal) jumps to her death over a precipice close to the monolith. Edith is running back towards the plain, and on the way down she sees (in the distance) the College mathematics teacher, Miss Greta McCraw. Miss McCraw, who is 45 years old, is on her way uphill, and is dressed only in her underclothes. Straight afterwards, Edith looks up through some branches and sees what she describes as "a funny sort of cloud" of "a nasty red colour".[5]

Edith being gone, Joan Lindsay writes (in the first paragraph of Chapter Eighteen) about "four people on the Rock". This means Miss McCraw, Miranda, Marion and Irma. We know that Irma returns from the Rock, and lives to be a countess whose dimple (when she smiles) is internationally famous. Thus, there is no simple meaning in Joan Lindsay's assurance that for Irma and the other three the events on Hanging Rock are going on happening "until the end of time". My own interpretation is that, at the end of Chapter Eighteen, the other three are dead; just as Irma, too, will be dead—well before "the end of time". The final chapter is not suggesting that the four of them could one day reappear alive on the Rock.

Earlier, when writing *The Murders at Hanging Rock*, I tackled the problem of interpreting the events described in the published version of *Picnic at Hanging Rock*. My five different interpretations were each of them as persuasive as possible and backed with detailed evidence from the book; but each of them contradicted the others because each was based on a different school of opinion about the universe we live in. At one extreme was the world of Hermetic magic — at the other, the materialist detective world. Chapter Eighteen poses a similar problem of interpretation; but this time I shall no longer be supporting Joan Lindsay's claim that the solution of the mystery is unimportant. Rather, I shall be looking for a single worldview that makes the chapter consistent within itself; thereby clarifying what is actually happening, and how the chapter relates to the rest of the book.

Chapter Eighteen's events are seen almost entirely from Irma's point of view; and Irma is excluded both from some of the sense-impressions her schoolgirl companions have, and from their understanding of what is happening. She does share, however, their inability to recognise Miss McCraw — an inability which cannot be explained by the fact that nobody from the College ever before saw the teacher scantily clad and without her glasses. Edith can easily recognise the same apparition by its peculiar shape — and confides that "Irma Leopold once told me, 'the McCraw is exactly the same shape as a flat iron' ".[6] Irma herself has lost the use of that former perception.

The "clown-woman" (whom the reader knows as Miss Greta McCraw) is viewed by the three girls as a "stranger"; and she claims to know neither her own name nor the girls' names (although we notice that, at the last, she uses the "girl Marion's" name without having heard either of the others use it). Irma, Marion and Miranda have no difficulty in remembering one another's names. As for their companion, I shall compromise between the "Greta McCraw" and the "clown-woman" aspects and call her, in future, "the McCraw".

Conversation resembles conversations in Lewis Carroll's *Through the Looking Glass* — the three girls playing the part of a visiting Alice, while the McCraw makes oracular pronouncements like a native inhabitant. Eventually, however, Irma alone is the Alice, or foreigner. In this region, Irma's presence is suffered (it seems) only because of the strength of the affection between herself and Miranda. Irma acquiesces in having her elegant French satin corset thrown over a cliff, not because she shares Marion's and Miranda's new consciousness — not because she has forgotten the world she later calls "home" — but rather because she has a frivolous disposition and is genuinely careless of her expensive belongings. She has no idea where the others are expecting to "arrive", but assumes she will go with them, simply because Marion and Miranda are her friends. She seems not to notice that no one includes her in the plan to enter the hole. If Michael Fitzhubert had not intervened, she might have waited outside, in bewilderment, for ever.

Three distinct regions are established here. Irma's aspirations and interests are grounded in the first of them — the world we all know. The second is the region of "colourless light" where Edith's screams are inaudible and the McCraw has no name. The third region is the ultimate experience, "the light", into which Irma's companions are able to pass.

The two unearthly regions could be translated in occult terms (the astral plane, and then Reintegration), or religiously (Purgatory and then Paradise, for example). However, remembering the McCraw's opinion that the corsets get "stuck fast in time", a more likely model is P. D. Ouspensky's treatment of time as having two extra dimensions which we do not perceive. The first of these extra dimensions is described as "the perpetual *now*" of every moment ever; the second extra dimension is the aggregate of all possibilities. Ouspensky writes that "if we attempt to unite the three co-ordinates of time into one whole we shall obtain a spiral".[7]

At the monolith, Marion and Miranda feel themselves being tugged by forces acting in the form of a spiral—a spiral which originates in the monolith, but has a different alignment from the vertical spirals that dowsers have claimed they sense at other monoliths. The force is not felt by Irma, and the twigs of nearby trees are unmoved by it; we must suppose that the force acts on susceptible consciousnesses, drawing them into a state appropriate to the two unearthly regions associated with what I shall now be calling Time Two and Time Three—the names that J. B. Priestley uses, in his adaptation of Ouspensky's model.

Priestley suggests that, after our physical death, we shall find our attention concentrated in Time Two, which "might well seem at first an uncontrollable dream world, through which our consciousness wanders like Alice on the other side of the looking glass".[8] This Time will contain "all the sensations, feelings, thoughts left to us from our Time-One lives", and experience there will partly resemble Purgatory.[9] Beyond purgation, we graduate to Time Three — white light, and the abandonment of individual personality. During our lifetime, some of us are aware only of our Time-One existence, although Priestley holds that our total self always exists in the other two Times as well. Marion and the McCraw, with their devotion to pure mathematics — Miranda, with her philosophical bent — are clearly more aware of abstract existence than the light-headed Irma is.

The first paragraph of Chapter Eighteen is the reason for identifying Time Two with the scene of the strange experiences that Irma never afterwards remembers. Marion, Miranda, Irma and the McCraw have entered this region without being dead; thus, their Time-One consciousness has continued to operate, not in the physical world, as it usually does, but in the region of what Ouspensky has called "perpetual *now*". This anomaly presumably makes it impossible to alter the "perpetual now" of these particular moments (whereas Priestley suggests that we may be able to alter the "now" of more normal moments, after we have died). Time-One consciousness is out of place in this region, where death of the physical body cannot extinguish it as Time-One consciousness is normally extinguished. Thus, the experience persists independently in Time Two, although the selves it should be part of may have advanced to Time Three, or may be conscious again in the physical world. This explains why the happenings on the Rock are particularised as invariable, and as existing in "a present without a past". The past that they lack is existence in the physical world.

This interpretation is impressively confusing; but it raises the very plain question of how the girls and the McCraw can be physically present in that kind of region. Even when people envisage these extra dimensions of time as if they were really space (in casual disguise), they do not expect them to be visitable by anything grosser than consciousness. It is the same when occultists envisage the astral plane; the physical body must stay elsewhere. But in *Picnic at Hanging Rock* the physical bodies have also left the everyday world.

Before presenting an explanation for this, I shall briefly dismiss certain other explanations. Chapter Eighteen shows that the lost people have not taken an unexpected direction and so discovered themselves to be in higher dimensional space; for one thing, they experience none of the curious visual effects associated with such an adventure. Nor is there justification for loose talk by people who have heard about the gravitational curvature of spacetime, and who have therefore postulated a mysterious gravitational effect associated with the Rock. Any gravitational effect that was extreme enough to account for the picnickers' disappearance (a short-lived small black hole, for example) would have such very disagreeable further effects — not only on the missing girls and governess but also on the Rock and its surroundings — that there would remain no Rock to be searched afterwards, and no picnic grounds; nor any picnicking schoolfellows to comment on anything odd. Similar objections apply to the notion that the pinkness observed by both Irma and Edith might be caused by gravity strong enough to alter the wavelength of light.

My own explanation of Chapter Eighteen's apparent anomalies will invoke the Australian Aboriginal model of the supernatural — which is translated in English as "the Dreaming". In a European occultist view, a human being's body may lie tranced or dreaming while the consciousness moves about in astral form, invisible to others. In the same way, we may suppose that the Australian landscape has an astral body for use in its Dreaming, and that the people and the Ancestors who appear in Dreaming legends are moving about in the landscape's astral consciousness, having been removed from its physical awareness. This has become the case for the girls and the McCraw. While they remain in the landscape's astral or Dreaming awareness, they are only virtual beings; they have no physical reality, any more than their oddly lit setting has.

In the "Bush Retribution" chapter of *The Murders at Hanging Rock* I quoted Jung's disclosure that "certain Australian primitives assert that one cannot conquer foreign soil because in it there dwell strange ancestor-spirits who reincarnate themselves in the newborn". This suggests that Miranda and Marion, in all ignorance, are each a human incarnation of an Australian Ancestor for whom, in Miranda's case, beetles are another form of incarnation, while Marion has a lizard for her totem. (We know their totems because a lizard approaches Marion in her sleep, while bronze beetles either tour around Miranda's head—in Chapter Eighteen—or trek across her ankle—in the altered Chapter Three.) In the Dreaming legend which tells of the Picnic adventure, we may suppose that a passing eagle let a mudcrab fall where the lizard and beetle were sleeping. (The legend would require the crab to be carried from a distance, since the McCraw's Ancestor-spirit would be Pictish, not Australian.) As the "Bush Retribution" chapter suggested, Irma's Jewishness prevents her having a totem, and perhaps also explains the final emphasis on the fact that her "soft" little hands are "white": perhaps this defines her again as unAboriginal — a foreigner.

The dreams of our landscape are strange, and they complicate the already dreamlike nature of Time Two, which is a part of them. A pink cloud (or pink smoke) is introduced to mark a boundary with physical reality; within the region of the cloud (as in legendary fairy kingdoms) time passes at a different rate, so that although Edith sets off running as fast as she can (before the others have even reached the monolith) she does not arrive at the picnic grounds until the search for the McCraw has been under way for an hour. (Presumably the position of the astral boundary alters, so that Edith runs at first in the physical world, and then in the astral consciousness until the pink cloud passes by.)

The spectacle of corsets "stuck fast in time" is partly a dreamlike confusion between sequences of events and spacetime mapped on a piece of paper; but "time" has also become a name for something gluey—like the "viscous sea" which Michael Fitzhubert dreams that he struggles through in his quest for Miranda (really a quest to wake the landscape up again). As in other dreams, there are several kinds of meaning for what is seen and said; the corsets could also be stuck in time because they are a short-lived fashion historically. We should hardly be surprised, moreover, if the McCraw had explained that a corset remains where it is because another word for corset is "stays"; there definitely is a rebus effect in this dream—as if it imitated puzzles where "hear" is represented by the letter "h" with a picture of an ear. (Possibly her students would often refer to the McCraw as "an old crab".) A rebus-model accounts for the brain full of intelligence and the heart full of understanding that the McCraw claims to perceive; and for the hole through which the picnickers will pass, having first been shown the real hole that is Buddhism's positive nothingness: a statement about reality, and a portent of Time Three.

The McCraw's mind has long

occupied itself, not with egotism, but with the world of Forms; and her merely physical form has meant so little to her that she readily prepares a way for Marion and Miranda by transforming into a crab. They are following a snake into a hole which has a lip rimmed with "bruised, heart-shaped leaves"; the rebus here shades into Freudian symbolism, as if the birth-canal is being re-entered to allow another birth into another world. Irma is left behind as a creature merely of curls and embroidery, who thinks of the physical world as "home" (whereas Miranda has lost all concern or regret for the friends and family she is bereaving).

The boulder crashes down over the hole; that is, the landscape's consciousness has surfaced again in the waking physical world, and virtual being has collapsed into reality. Michael Fitzhubert's intervention has done this. Irma and her setting are suddenly physical again; and so are the bodies of Miranda, Marion and the McCraw. True to the image produced later by hysterical girls at the College, the lost people now "lie rotting in a filthy cave"—a cave which they could never have entered except in the Dreaming state of the landscape. The Dreaming events have spared them the purgatorial stretch in Time Two which Priestley has predicted for most of us; their passage into Time Three has been relatively painless.

Clearly, Chapter Eighteen has not explained the mystery away into trivialities, as some people have feared it might. We still do not know what the landscape did with the McCraw's outer garments and with Irma's shoes and stockings. We wonder whether Irma's ringlets and bodice got bloodstained because blood dripped from Michael Fitzhubert's injured forehead, as he leaned over her in a scene that has stayed unrecorded. And perhaps it was light-hearted minor spirits of the bushland who stopped people's watches at the Picnic?

The film and the published novel of *Picnic at Hanging Rock* are complete in their present form; each, in different ways, an evocation of the Australian bushland, and of the Rock's curious fascination. Whatever Chapter Eighteen was like, its publication could never have reduced their haunting quality. As it is, the chapter adds to the Hanging Rock mystique. Joan Lindsay's original intention is finally disclosed — but her intention was not to dissolve the mystery. The *Picnic* geography is clarified, but the eeriness remains.

NOTES

1. Joan Lindsay, *Picnic at Hanging Rock*, Penguin, Harmondsworth, 1970, p. 106.
2. Lindsay, p. 39.
3. Lindsay, p. 38.
4. Lindsay, p. 39.
5. Lindsay, p. 64.
6. Lindsay, p. 66.
7. Quoted in J. B. Priestley, *Man and Time*, Aldus Books, London, 1964, p. 267.
8. Priestley, pp. 302-4.
9. Priestley, p. 302.

JOAN LINDSAY

The daughter of Mr Justice Theyre a'Beckett Weigall, Joan Lindsay was born in 1896 in St Kilda, Victoria. Through the a'Beckett family Joan Lindsay was related to the Boyds, a family of artists and writers. Through her marriage to Daryl Lindsay she joined another family of artists and writers. Her publications include *Picnic at Hanging Rock, Time Without Clocks, Facts Soft and Hard, Syd Sixpence* and *Through Darkest Pondelayo* (written under the pseudonym Serena Livingstone-Stanley). Joan Lindsay died in 1984.

JOHN TAYLOR

A Sydney writer, editor, lecturer and critic, John Taylor was educated in various libraries and at the East Sydney Technical College Cooking School. He has written a children's book, *Happyendia*, a play about Rasputin and articles for *The Teaching of English* and *Adventist News* (about Lindy Chamberlain's innocence) as well as editing or reviewing hundreds of books. He appears on the ABC radio programme "Science Bookshop".

YVONNE ROUSSEAU

A Melbourne short-story writer and book-reviewer, Yvonne Rousseau is the author of *The Murders at Hanging Rock*.